SCIENCE
MAKERS

Making with
LIGHT

Anna Claybourne

BUILD **AMAZING PROJECTS** WITH
INSPIRATIONAL SCIENTISTS,
ARTISTS AND **ENGINEERS**

First published in Great Britain in 2018 by Wayland
Copyright © Hodder and Stoughton, 2018
All rights reserved.

Editor: Sarah Silver
Designer: Eoin Norton
Picture researcher: Diana Morris

ISBN 978 1 5263 0526 8

All photographs by Eoin Norton for Wayland except the following:
Antagain/istockphoto: 25b. © Caitlind r.c. Brown & Wayne Garrett. Photo Mica Radek/AFP/
Getty Images: 5b. © Vicki DaSilva Visual Artist. vickidasilva.com. lightgraffiti.com: 20tl, 20tr.
Courtesy of the artist, Tracey Emin: 26t. © Tracey Emin. All rights reserved, DACS/Artimage
2017. Image courtesy Lehmann Maupin: 26b. Everett Historical/Shutterstock: 5tl. Oliver
Hoffmann/Shutterstock: 14bl. Alex Hubanov/Shutterstock: 23bl. de Larmessin/Wikimedia
Commons: 8tl. Kevin Lavorgna/Shutterstock: 5tr. J.L.Lovell. University of Massachusetts
Amherst: 10tl. maxpro/Shutterstock: 4t. Courtesy NGA Washington: 18tr. Nikada/istockphoto:
29t. PD/Wikimedia Commons: 18tl. pixelklex/Shutterstock: 21bl. Jeroen Rouwema/Wikimedia
Commons: 12br. Scala/Superstock: 22tl. Science History Images/Alamy: 12cl, 16tl. Sherpa03/
Dreamstime: 22tr. vladee/Shutterstock: 29b. Courtesy of the artist, Jeff Wall: 24tl.
© Jeff Wall, A Sudden Gust of Wind (after Hokusai) 1993 transparency in
lightbox, 229.0 x 377.0. Courtesy of the artist: 24tr. Wellcome Library/Wikimedia
Commons: 13t. © Kumi Yamashita. Courtesy of the artist.: 6tl, 6tr.

Every attempt has been made to clear copyright. Should there be any
inadvertent omission please apply to the publisher for rectification.

Printed in China

Wayland, an imprint of
Hachette Children's Group
Part of Hodder and Stoughton
Carmelite House
50 Victoria Embankment
London EC4Y 0DZ

An Hachette UK Company
www.hachette.co.uk
www.hachettechildrens.co.uk

Note:
In preparation of this book, all due care has been exercised with regard to the instructions, activities
and techniques depicted. The publishers regret that they can accept no liability for any loss or injury
sustained. Always follow manufacturers' advice when using electric and battery-powered appliances.

The website addresses (URLs) included in this book were valid at the time of going to press.
However, because of the nature of the Internet, it is possible that some addresses may have
changed, or sites may have changed or closed down since publication. While the author
and publishers regret any inconvenience this may cause to the readers, no responsibility
for any such changes can be accepted by either the author or the publishers.

CONTENTS

TAKE CARE!

These projects can be made with everyday objects, materials and tools that you can find at home, or in a supermarket, hobby store or DIY store. However, some do involve working with things that are sharp or breakable, or need extra strength to operate. Make sure you have an adult on hand to supervise and to help with anything that could be dangerous, and get permission before you try out any of the projects.

UNDERSTANDING LIGHT

The sun is a star that gives out a huge amount of light energy. Without it, most life on Earth could not exist.

Light is incredibly important for all of us. Light energy coming from the sun gives us daylight and warmth, powers the weather, and helps plants grow, providing food for animals and humans. We use artificial lights to help us do things at night. And we use light in many machines, from tablets, cameras and film projectors to laser printers and solar-powered cars.

WHAT IS LIGHT?

Light can actually be quite hard to understand, and has puzzled scientists for centuries. It's basically a form of energy that travels at a very high speed, and can move across empty space. It is made up of energy waves, and has a range of different wavelengths. Different colours of light have different wavelengths.

Light energy comes in a wide spectrum of wavelengths, from very long to very short.

Long-wavelength light includes radio waves and microwaves.

Most wavelengths are invisible to us. The only light we can see is the medium-wavelength light in the middle.

Short-wavelength light includes x-rays.

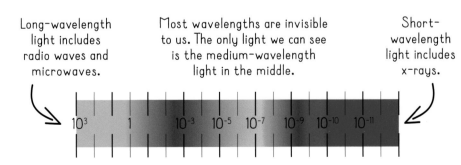

10^3 1 10^{-3} 10^{-5} 10^{-7} 10^{-9} 10^{-10} 10^{-11}

Visible light ranges from longer-wavelength red light to shorter-wavelength violet light.

American inventor Thomas Edison (1847–1931), is often credited with inventing the lightbulb, but in fact many different inventors contributed to the idea.

LIGHT INVENTIONS

Using light to make and invent things has been going on for a very long time. Prehistoric monuments such as Stonehenge (right) were built to line up with the sunrise at particular times of year, working as a kind of calendar. Mirrors, shadow clocks and lamps have existed since ancient times. And some of the most important inventions in history have been light-based, including the lightbulb, photography, microscopes and telescopes, fibre optics and solar power.

A sculpture named *Cloud*, on display in Brno in the Czech Republic in 2014. Created by Canadian artists Caitlind r.c. Brown and Wayne Garrett, it's made of hundreds of lightbulbs.

ART AND LIGHT

Of course, light has always been essential for visual artists. Painters, such as Caravaggio (1571–1610), used light and shade to create lifelike masterpieces. Film, electric light and photography are being used more and more by artists to make changing, interactive works.

ART IN
SHADOWS

SHADOWS

Create your own artworks by playing around with light and shadow.

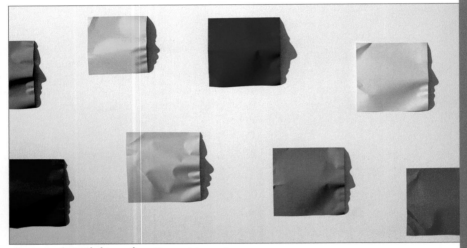

Origami (2012) (detail) © Kumi Yamashita

> I sculpt using light and shadow.
> I construct single or multiple objects and place them in relation to a single light source. The complete artwork is therefore composed of both the material (the solid objects) and the immaterial (the light or shadow).
> – *Kumi Yamashita*

MAKER PROFILE:

Kumi Yamashita
(1968–)

New York-based Japanese artist Kumi Yamashita creates light and shadow sculptures from everyday objects.

At first glance, her work may appear to be the silhouettes of people, but look closely and they are actually sheets of paper attached to walls. She also uses an assortment of wood blocks, fabrics and steel plates to create the sculptures.

She shines light on these at just the right angle, which transforms them into extraordinary works of art.

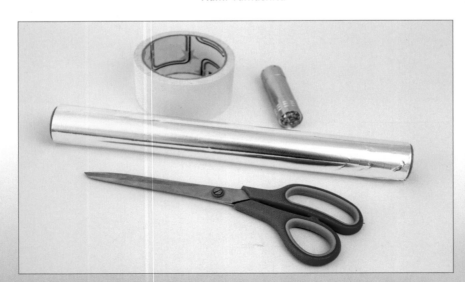

WHAT YOU NEED

- aluminium foil
- scissors
- masking tape
- torch
- a wall to display your art on

1.

Step 1.
Cut out or fold a sheet of aluminium foil into a rectangle, no smaller than 30 cm x 20 cm.

2.

Step 2.
Use one edge of the foil to shape the portrait. Crease the foil into peaks to form sticking out parts like the nose and chin. Create different shapes along the edge that will form the outline of your portrait.

3.

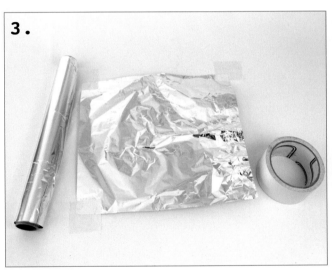

Step 3.
Use a piece of masking tape on the corners of the sheet and attach the sheet to the wall.

4.

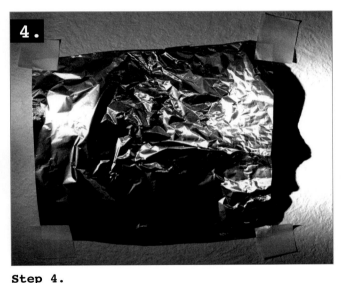

Step 4.
Turn the lights down and shine the torch light towards your sheet. Move it around until you get the angle that shows off your portrait to its best effect.

CASTING SHADOWS

Shadows are made when an object blocks light. Light travels in straight lines, so it can't curve around the object. Instead, it leaves a dark area in the shape of the object. However, the shape of a shadow can be stretched, depending on the angle the light is coming from. Shining the light from the side makes the small shapes in the edge of the foil cast longer shadows.

SUNDOWN SHADOWS

The same thing happens with your own shadow. At midday, when the sun is high overhead, your shadow is short. In the evening, when the sun is low down near the horizon, your shadow is much longer.

⌜A NEW VIEW⌟

See around corners or over walls with this old but brilliant invention.

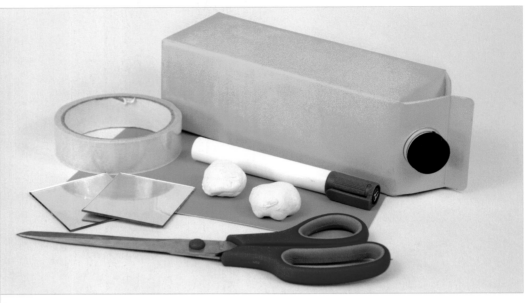

MAKER PROFILE:

Johannes Gutenberg
(c. 1398–1468)

German inventor Johannes Gutenberg lived in the 1400s. He is most famous for developing the printing press in about 1440. Before that, though, in the 1430s, he's thought to have made the first periscopes to help people to see over the crowds at religious shrines and festivals!

WHAT YOU NEED

- two small mirrors, available from craft stores or chemists
- a long, rectangular cardboard box that's slightly wider than your mirrors (such as a fruit juice carton)
- sticky tack
- scissors
- marker pen
- piece of paper
- sticky tape

1.

Step 1.
To make the periscope, you'll need to cut open one of the wider sides of the box. If necessary, tape any other openings closed.

Step 2.
Draw two squares on the narrower sides of the box, one at one end, and one at the other end on the opposite side. Cut them out.

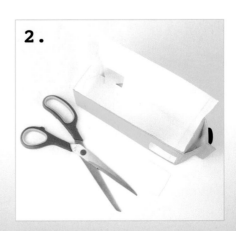
2.

Step 3.

Fold over a corner of your paper to make a 45° angle. Cut the corner off and put it inside one end of the box, in the corner, with the sloping angle facing one of the holes. Draw along the edge to mark the angle for the mirror. Turn the box around and do the same at the other end.

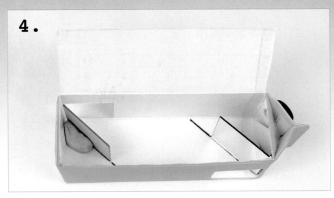

Step 4.

Roll two large lumps of sticky tack, and stick them to the backs of the two mirrors. Press the mirrors into place in the ends of the box so that their reflecting surfaces line up with the lines you have drawn.

Step 5.

Close the side of the box and check your periscope by looking into the hole at the bottom end. You may need to adjust the mirrors a little. You should be able to look into one end and see out of the other!

Step 6.

Once you're sure your periscope works, use sticky tape to close the open side of the box. You can also paint or decorate it.

SEEING AROUND A CORNER

A periscope lets you see around a corner or over a wall – or over a crowd, as Gutenberg intended – by changing the direction of light rays. It works because light bounces, or reflects, off mirrors at the same angle as it hits the mirror.

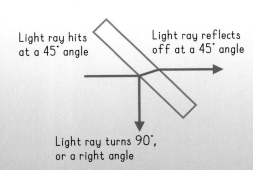

Light ray hits at a 45° angle

Light ray reflects off at a 45° angle

Light ray turns 90°, or a right angle

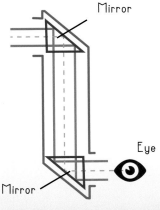

Mirror

Eye

Mirror

A periscope uses two mirrors to collect light at one end of the box, and bounce it out at the other. When it reaches your eyes, they see the view from the other end of the box.

Periscopes are also used in submarines to look out above the water surface.

CURVED LIGHT

Honour the inventor of fibre optic tubes with your own homemade fibre optic lamp.

MAKER PROFILE:

William Wheeler
(1851–1932)

William Wheeler was an American engineer and teacher who used pipes to build water supply systems. In 1880, he tried using pipes to carry light instead. He designed a set of linked glass tubes with a reflective coating. Light could be shone into one end, then carried along the pipes and around corners to any room in a house, using reflection. This was one of the first steps towards the invention of modern fibre-optic cables.

Be it known that I, WILLIAM WHEELER ... have invented a new and useful Improvement in Apparatus for Lighting Dwellings.
– William Wheeler

WHAT YOU NEED

- at least 3 m of clear, stretchy beading thread (more if you like, up to about 10 m)
- a piece of cardboard
- paper cup
- scissors
- sticky tape
- sticky tack
- a bright mini LED torch, shorter than your paper cup
- aluminium foil

Step 1.
Have a piece of sticky tape ready, about 10 cm long. Wind about 3 to 10 m of beading thread around a piece of card.

Step 2.
Remove the bundle of thread from the card and wind the piece of tape around one end of it.

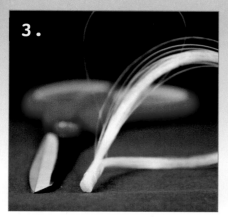

Step 3.
Cut off the shorter end of the bundle neatly, so that the ends of the thread are all lined up together, and held in place by the tape.

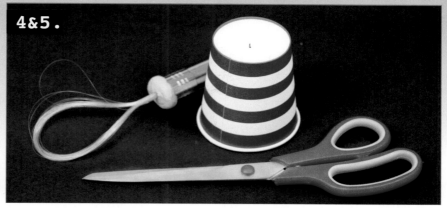

Step 4.
Roll the sticky tack tightly around the taped end of the thread and then push this firmly onto the end of your torch so that no light shows through.

Step 5.
Use the scissors to make a hole in the bottom of the cup, as wide as your bundle of thread.

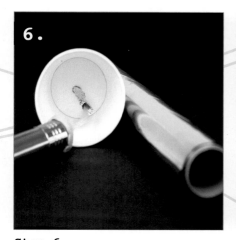

Step 6.
Fold the bundle of thread and put some foil over the top end (this makes it easier to thread them). Thread the bundle through the hole in the cup, from the inside.

Step 7.
Gently push the torch up inside the cup and remove the foil from the the thread. Cut through the loop with scissors so that the threads spray out in all directions.

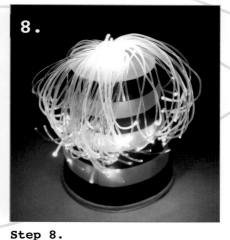

Step 8.
Switch on the torch and take your fibre-optic lamp to a dark room. The light should be carried to the ends of the threads, appearing as shining dots.

INTERNAL REFLECTION

Wheeler's lighting tubes and your fibre optic lamp both work using 'internal reflection' – light moving along inside a curving tube by reflecting to and fro.

It only works if light can bounce off the inside of the tube. Wheeler made his glass tubes extra-reflective by coating them with silver. Modern glass fibre optic cables are similar, but much smaller and very flexible. With the beading thread, a little bit of light does escape – but enough is reflected to carry a point of light to the end of each one.

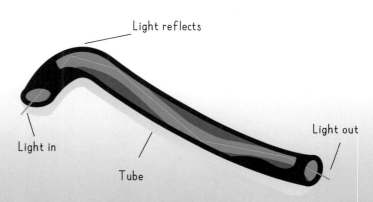

Light reflects

Light in

Tube

Light out

A CLOSER LOOK

Make a microscope like brilliant scientist Antonie van Leeuwenhoek, and discover a hidden world!

MAKER PROFILE:

Antonie van Leeuwenhoek
(1632–1723)

Dutch shopkeeper and scientist Antonie van Leeuwenhoek sold cloth, and used magnifying glasses to inspect fabrics. By heating and melting glass, he managed to make tiny glass spheres that worked as super-powerful magnifiers. He mounted each sphere in a metal plate, making the first microscopes.

Van Leeuwenhoek soon realised there was a lot more to look at in close-up than just cloth. In fact, his invention led him to discover microbes – tiny living things such as bacteria. He called them 'animalcules'.

I then most always saw, with great wonder, that in the said matter there were many very little living animalcules, very prettily a-moving.
– Antonie van Leeuwenhoek

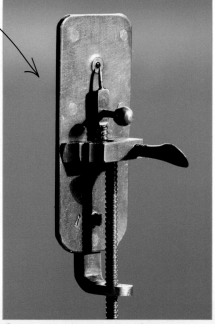

One of van Leeuwenhoek's own microscopes.

William Heath's cartoon *Monster Soup*, c. 1928, shows a woman looking through a miscroscope to discover the supposed impurity of the River Thames in London.

WHAT YOU NEED

- a piece of card
- a piece of clear acetate
- scissors
- sticky tape
- large, sharp needle
- wooden skewer
- petroleum jelly
- a small bowl and some water
- two paper cups
- small glass
- objects to look at, such as feathers, leaves or flowers

Step 1.
Cut a rectangular hole in the middle of your card. Cut a piece of acetate the same shape as the hole, but slightly larger all round.

Step 2.
Place the acetate over the hole, and fix the edges in place with sticky tape. Use the needle to carefully make a hole in the middle of the acetate.

Step 3.
Smear some petroleum jelly onto the pointed end of the wooden skewer, and push it through the hole. This will make the hole bigger and add an oily barrier around it.

Step 4.
Stand the card on the two cups or cans so that the hole is in the middle with nothing underneath it. Fill the bowl with water and dip the cocktail stick or skewer into it.

Step 5.
Carefully drip drops of water into the tiny hole.

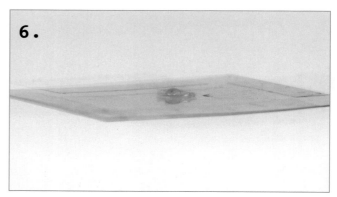

Step 6.
You should end up with a drop of water sitting in the hole. If it doesn't work or you get water everywhere, gently clean it off with kitchen roll and try again.

The drop of water works like the tiny round glass ball in van Leeuwenhoek's version.

Step 7.
To use the microscope, turn your glass upside down and put your object (such as a leaf) on top of it. Slide it carefully under the water drop.

8.

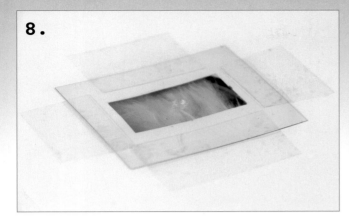

Shut one eye and use the other to look as closely as you can at the water drop. Press down gently on the card to get it at just the right distance, and you should see your object magnified.

LENSES AND LIGHT

The round water drop works as a lens — a curved, clear object that bends light by refraction. As light passes between the air and the water, the change in material makes the light rays bend, or refract. When the bent light reaches your eye, it makes the object you are looking at appear much bigger, and you can see tiny details.

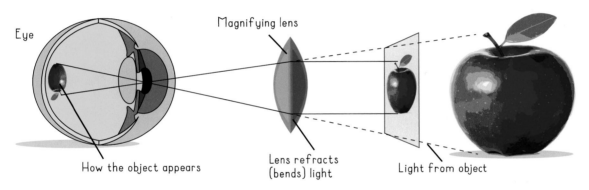

Eye

Magnifying lens

How the object appears

Lens refracts (bends) light

Light from object

A normal magnifying glass works the same way, but its lens is flatter and less powerful. Van Leeuwenhoek found that a very small sphere makes light refract much more. A water drop isn't a perfect sphere, but it's almost as good (and easier to make!).

TRY THIS!

If you have a smartphone, you may be able to line up the camera lens on the phone with the water drop, allowing you to see the images more clearly and take photos of them.

There's another method too — but only try this if you have permission (and only with an old phone). Also, only do this with a lens that's covered in glass and not close to the phone's microphone. Hold the phone with its camera facing up, and use your finger to drip a small water drop directly over the middle of the lens.

Carefully turn the phone over with a semicircular movement, so that the drop stays in place. You can then use the phone's camera as a microscope to look at and photograph things in close-up! (It may take a few attempts to get it right.)

MAKE THE WORLD UPSIDE DOWN

Build your own camera and see how the eye works by following in the footsteps of an inventive science maker.

MAKER PROFILE:

Ibn al-Haytham
(965–1040)

This pioneering scientist made key discoveries about the nature of sight.

He was the first person to prove, through experiments, that light travels in straight lines and bounces off objects. To aid his investigations, he invented a chamber known as a 'camera obscura'. It was a dark room, with a tiny opening to let in light. Ibn al-Haytham found that this captured an image of the world outside, which appeared upside-down on the opposite wall. This also helped him prove that vision occurs when light enters the eye, rather than from the eye emitting light as was commonly believed.

WHAT YOU NEED

- empty cylindrical crisp tube
- tracing paper
- pencil or marker pen
- ruler
- sharp knife
- scissors
- drawing pin or noticeboard pin
- strong sticky tape
- aluminium foil

1.

Step 1.
Take the plastic lid off the cylindrical crisp tube – but don't throw it away! Draw a line with the pencil all the way round the tube, about 5 cm up from the bottom.

Step 2.
Ask an adult to use the knife to cut along the line so the tube is in two pieces.

2.

3.

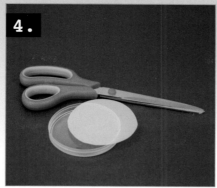

4.

Step 3.
The shorter piece has a metal end. With adult help, make a hole in the centre of the metal with a drawing pin.

Step 4.
Cut out a piece of tracing paper that just fits inside the lid of the crisp tube and place it inside the lid. It should fit tightly so it doesn't fall out when tipped up. This will act as a screen.

5.

6.

Step 5.
Put the lid onto the top of the shorter piece of the tube. Join the two pieces of tube together using sticky tape.

Step 6.
Tape one end of the aluminium foil to the tube. Wrap the foil all the way round the tube twice, and tape down the end. This will keep light out of the tube.

7.

Step 7.
The viewer will work best on a bright, sunny day. Outside, or at a bright window, close one eye and hold the tube up to your eye. You want the inside of the tube to be as dark as possible, so cup your hands around the opening of the tube if you need to.

As you look through the tube, you'll see the world upside down!

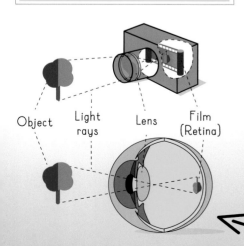

Object   Light rays   Lens   Film (Retina)

YOUR EYE AS CAMERA

The upside-down viewer is a type of camera obscura, like al-Haytham's dark room. When light rays pass through the pinhole, they cross over to the opposite side. This creates an upside-down image of the outside world on the screen. Cameras and the human eye work in the same way.

SUN PRINTS

Use the sun to capture images of everyday and natural objects, like photography pioneer Thomas Wedgwood.

MAKER PROFILE:

Thomas Wedgwood
(1771–1805)

Thomas Wedgwood came from a famous pottery-making family, and was both an art lover and a science experimenter. He was especially interested in light and images. In the 1790s, he found a way to capture an image of an object, such as a piece of lace or a leaf. He put an object on paper or on leather coated with silver nitrate, a light-sensitive chemical, and left them in the sun. Where the sunlight reached the paper, it changed it to a darker colour. Where it was blocked by the object, a lighter image remained.

The images, which Wedgwood called 'sun prints' or 'sun pictures', were a type of early photograph. But Wedgwood couldn't find a way to fix them – daylight would eventually turn the paper black all over. The prints could only be preserved by keeping them in the dark. It would be many more years before permanent photos were invented.

There are two ways of making sun prints, depending on which type of paper you have. You could try both and compare them.

WHAT YOU NEED

- everyday flattish objects such as flowers, leaves, keys, string, coins, buttons and beads
- a sunny windowsill or any other safe, sunny spot
- dark-coloured sugar paper or construction paper, or specially made sun print paper from a toy or hobby store
- a tray and a container of water (if using sun print paper)

THE SUGAR PAPER METHOD:

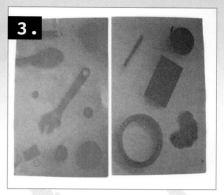

Step 1.
Spread out a sheet of sugar paper in your sunny spot. It needs to be somewhere where it won't get moved or disturbed by the wind, pets or little brothers or sisters!

Step 2.
Arrange a selection of objects on the paper to make a pattern, design or picture. Then leave the paper in the sun for as long as you can – all day, if possible.

Step 3.
Remove the objects and look at your print. Sunlight fades the paper, making it paler. Where the objects were, you'll see a darker image.

THE SUN PRINT PAPER METHOD:

Step 1.
Sun print paper is much more light-sensitive, so you have to work faster. Remove one piece of paper from the pack (and re-close the pack tightly). Put the paper on the tray, blue side up, and arrange your objects on it.

Step 2.
Move the tray into the sunlight and wait until the paper around the objects has turned white or very pale blue. In bright sunlight, this should only take two minutes. If it's less sunny, it will take longer, up to half an hour.

Step 3.
Move the tray out of the sun. Quickly remove the objects and put the paper into the water. Leave it there for at least a minute to develop, then take it out and leave to dry. You will now have a fixed pale image on a darker background.

COLOUR CHANGES

There are several substances that are sensitive to bright light. Sunlight breaks down the ink in the sugar paper, making it fade. You'll see the same effect on curtains or a poster that's been in the sun for a long time – the colours fade.

Sun print paper is coated with chemicals that react to light. When the paper is soaked in water, the parts exposed to the light become darker, creating a clear image of the objects.

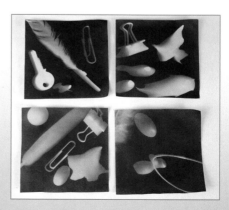

PAINTING WITH

Make your own 'light graffiti' like pioneering artist Vicki DaSilva.

MAKER PROFILE:

Vicki DaSilva
(1960–)

American artist Vicki DaSilva uses the technique of light painting, or 'light graffiti', as she sometimes calls her work. Wearing a dark outfit, she moves large fluorescent lamps around to make patterns, pictures or messages, against a backdrop of a room, building, landscape or sometimes a famous landmark. When captured using a camera with a long exposure, this creates a striking light painting. She's made light paintings in all kinds of places, from beaches, art galleries and city streets to the Eiffel Tower and the White House. Although DaSilva uses only professional cameras for her work, you can give it a go using a smartphone with a long exposure app.

> This light graffiti ... this legal graffiti ... this medium where I can go anywhere, and write anything.
> – *Vicki DaSilva*

Vicki DaSilva slows down and speeds up her light source to give texture to her works, as in this light painting, *East River Esplanade #3*, 2014.

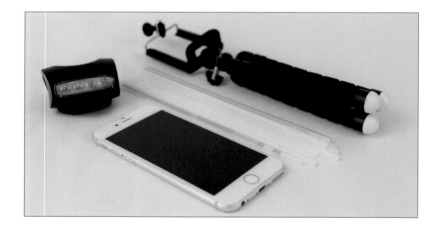

WHAT YOU NEED

- a smartphone or tablet with a camera
- an app that allows you to take long exposures, such as Slow Shutter Cam, NightCap or LongExpo (always ask whoever pays before buying an app)
- light sources, such as glow sticks, toys with flashing lights, or a small torch
- a smartphone tripod, if possible

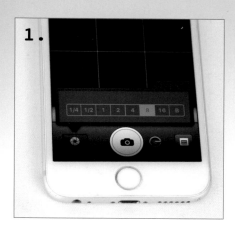

Step 1.

First you'll need to download your app and try out the settings, to work out how to set the exposure time. An exposure time of about 10 seconds is good to start with.

Step 2.

Set up your phone or tablet somewhere quite dark – it could be a room with the lights off, or a dark garden. If possible, use a tripod to hold it still. If you don't have a tripod, ask someone to operate the phone or tablet while resting it on a table or fixed surface.

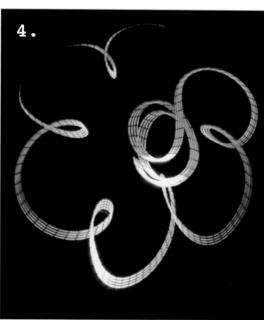

Step 3.

Get your light sources ready and stand in view of the camera. Start the long exposure shot, and while it is running, use the light sources to draw shapes, patterns or words in the air.

Step 4.

When the shot is finished, check out your picture. You should be able to see an image made up of the lines of light you have drawn. Experiment with different camera settings, light sources and styles, and save and print the pictures you like most.

As well as abstract shapes, you can 'paint' words and objects.

LIGHT TRAILS

A digital camera is sensitive to light. For a normal photo, the camera records light only for a split second, to give a sharp image of a single moment. A longer exposure, lasting several seconds, collects all the light that enters the camera during that time.

Normally, this would just give you a blurry image. But in the dark, it will record a moving light as a line or mark, like a brush stroke. Keeping the light source in one place or moving it slowly will result in a stronger glow, while moving it faster will make a fainter line.

GARDEN GNOMON

Build your own ancient-Greek-style shadow clock in a garden or on the beach.

MAKER PROFILE:

Anaximander
(c. 610–546 BCE)

Anaximander was an ancient Greek philosopher and scientist. He experimented with many things, including the gnomon, a stick stuck into the ground to cast a shadow. You can use a gnomon as a kind of clock, and also to map the seasons and solstices.

Anaximander didn't invent the gnomon — they existed long before his time, in ancient Sumeria and other places, such as ancient China. But he did design and build his own gnomons, and introduced them to ancient Greece.

If you don't have a garden to use, you might be able to make a gnomon in a school playground or on the beach (see right). This project will work best in summer, and if you are not close to the equator.

WHAT YOU NEED

- a large, strong, straight stick at least 1 m long
- 12 stones
- a sunny spot in a garden where your gnomon won't be disturbed
- a bucket of sand or bark chips (optional)
- a clock or watch
- marker pen

Step 1.
Ask an adult to make a hole in the ground and push the stick into it. If this isn't possible, you can stand the stick in a bucket and fill it with bark chips or sand to hold the stick upright.

Step 2.
Wait until your clock or watch shows a time on the hour, such as 6 a.m. Put a stone on the shadow of the gnomon, and write a number 6 on the stone with a marker pen.

Step 3.
Check the gnomon every hour, and add a stone to show where the shadow is for each hour, making a curved line of stones. It may take a few days to do this, if it isn't always sunny.

Step 4.
You can now use your gnomon as a clock, looking at where the shadow falls to see what time it is.

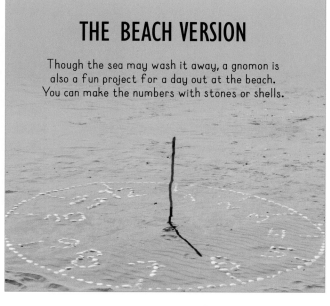

THE BEACH VERSION

Though the sea may wash it away, a gnomon is also a fun project for a day out at the beach. You can make the numbers with stones or shells.

SHADOW CLOCKS

A gnomon is one of the simplest and oldest clocks there is. It works because the Earth rotates once a day, making the sun appear in different positions in the sky. This means that shadows fall in different places at different times.

However, a simple gnomon isn't very accurate, because as summer becomes winter, the sun moves across a smaller part of the sky, and the shadows won't be in quite the same places. After Anaximander, other scientists improved the gnomon by making the stick lean over at an angle that matches the axis of the Earth. The sundials you see in gardens are usually at an angle. This makes the shadows for each hour fall in the same places, whatever the time of year.

LIGHT BOX DISPLAY

Make your own light box to display a moveable message or a work of art.

MAKER PROFILE:

Jeff Wall
(1946–)

Early in his career, Canadian photography artist Jeff Wall was inspired by the way large advertising hoardings were often lit from behind, drawing attention to the glowing images. He decided to display some of his pictures in the same way, mounting them on huge light boxes, and these are now his most famous works.

A light box is a wide, shallow box with a translucent surface, lit from inside. Artists and designers often use them to work on, helping them to see detail and colour clearly. They have also become a popular room decoration, and come with letters or pictures that you can arrange on the front.

Jeff Wall, *A Sudden Gust of Wind (after Hokusai)*, 1993, transparency in lightbox, 229.0 x 377.0. Courtesy of the artist.

Many of Jeff Wall's artworks are photographs of carefully set-up scenes, either remembered from real life, or recreated from paintings.

WHAT YOU NEED

- a shallow, sturdy cardboard box with a separate lid, such as a chocolate box
- a set of small battery-powered fairy lights
- two sheets of clear acetate
- tracing paper
- pencil
- ruler
- scissors or craft knife
- invisible sticky tape

- marker pens, or a computer and printer

Step 1.
Using the pencil and ruler, lightly draw a frame on the front of the box, about 1 cm in from the edge. Ask an adult to use scissors or a craft knife to cut out the middle as neatly as possible.

Step 2.
Turn the lid over and measure the dimensions inside it. Measure out and cut two pieces of acetate and four pieces of tracing paper the same size, so that they will fit neatly inside.

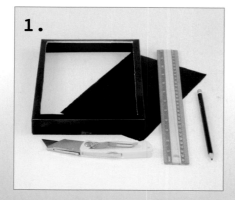
1.

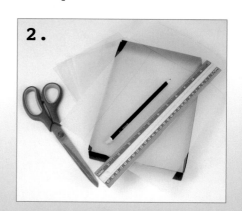
2.

3.

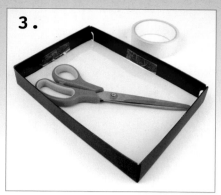

Step 3.
First put a piece of acetate into the lid, then all the tracing paper pieces, then another piece of acetate. Press them all down and use sticky tape to fix them firmly to the inside of the lid.

4.

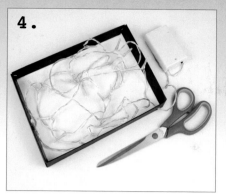

Step 4.
Put the lid aside. Use the scissors to cut a slot about 1 cm wide in the box itself, low down on one side. Put the fairy lights into the box, with the wire leading out though the slot, so that the battery pack and switch are outside the box.

5.

Step 5.
Press the fairy lights gently down into the box and secure them to the base, by sticking down the cable between each light with pieces of tape. Put the lid on and switch on the lights to see your light box in action.

6.

Step 6.
To display a photograph or artwork on your light box, you can either draw a picture directly onto a piece of tracing paper, or print out a photograph or artwork onto tracing paper. Trim it to the right size and tape it to the front of the light box to display it.

7 & 8.

Step 7.
To make a message light box, cut two strips of acetate, the same length as the box and about 1 cm wide. Use invisible tape to attach them to the front edges of the light box to create letter slots.

Step 8.
Use a computer to write large alphabet letters in an interesting font, and print them out onto tracing paper. Cut the printout into small rectangles, each with one letter on it. Slot the letters underneath the strips of acetate to spell a message.

WE ARE ALL MOTHS!

We know that moths are drawn towards light, but scientists have found that humans are too. In experiments, people will choose to sit facing a wall that is lit up, and will pay more attention to light that is moving or flashing, or contrasts strongly with a darker background. This is why light boxes, neon signs and flashing messages are effective ways of advertising.

DIFFUSE LIGHT!

A light box wouldn't work as well if there were lights behind clear glass or acetate. Instead, the light needs to be 'diffused', or spread and evened out, to make a gently glowing backdrop that doesn't interfere with the image. The DIY light box uses tracing paper to get this effect, as it's translucent – meaning it lets light through, but blurs it so you can't see a clear image. A professional light box uses translucent glass or plastic.

NEON SIGN

Make your own neon sign, to tell the world a message of your choice!

MAKER PROFILE:

Tracey Emin is a leading British artist who makes many different kinds of works, including paintings, drawing, sculptures and art installations. She often uses words and messages in her art, many of them in the form of lit-up neon signs. They combine the fun, exciting 'feel-good factor' of glowing colour with thoughtful or emotional words.

Tracey Emin
(1963–)

Emin's signs are made of glass and use neon gas, like the signs used on shops and theatres, but these are very difficult to make at home as it's hard to bend glass tubing. Instead, you can use a type of wire that lights up, called EL (electroluminescent) wire, to make your own realistic-looking neon sign.

Tracey Emin's neon sign artwork *Trust Yourself*, 2014.

> Being an artist isn't just about making nice things, or people patting you on the back; it's some kind of communication, a message.
> *– Tracey Emin*

WHAT YOU NEED

- pencil and paper
- a length of ready-to-use EL wire about 2-3 m long and 2-3 mm thick, with a battery pack attached (see panel below)
- batteries to fit the battery pack
- the same length of bendable garden wire
- pliers
- wire cutters (these are often part of the pliers)
- clear or invisible sticky tape

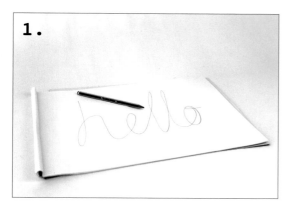

Step 1.

First, decide on what you want to write. 2-3 m of wire should be enough for one word or a short two-word phrase. Sketch out how you would like it to look, remembering that all the letters will have to be connected.

EL wire is often sold as a ready-to-use kit with a battery pack and switch already included. It comes in lots of different colours and widths, and some have flashing options too. You can find it in hobby and electronics stores, or online (see page 31). Before making your sign, insert the batteries and check your wire works.

Step 2.

With an adult to help, cut off a piece of garden wire the same length as your EL wire. Use the pliers to bend over the sharp ends and squeeze them in tightly, so they don't scratch you while you're working.

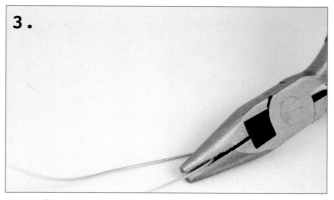

Step 3.

Now start to gently bend and shape the garden wire to make your word. It can be tricky, so ask an adult to help if necessary. To make sharp corners, hold the wire tightly in the pliers and bend it close to where the pliers are holding it.

4.

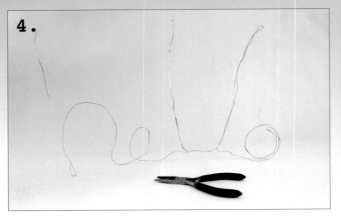

Step 4.

When your word is finished, press it against a hard surface to make it as flat as possible. Cut off any excess garden wire and fold the cut end over again so that it's not sharp.

5.

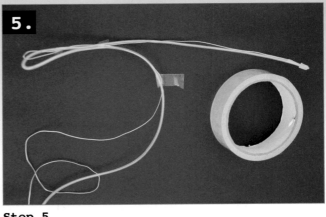

Step 5.

Now you can attach the EL wire. Start at the loose end of the wire, not the battery end. Carefully line up the EL wire with the garden wire, bit by bit, and attach them together using small pieces of sticky tape. Once the sign is lit up, they will be almost invisible.

6.

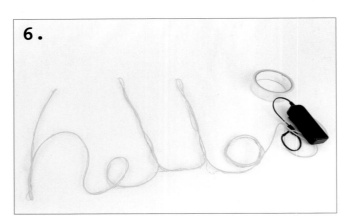

Step 6.

As you work, make sure you are keeping the EL wire on top of the garden wire all the way along. At the end, use extra tape to make an extra-strong join where the garden wire ends and the EL wire extends and leads to the battery pack.

WHAT TO WRITE

Stuck for ideas? How about …

- Your favourite band, song or sport
  - A pet's name
  - A message to the world, like 'Be happy!'

Step 7.

Switch on the EL wire to see the sign lit up! You can now stand it on a shelf or mantlepiece to display it. Place the battery pack and any spare wire off to one side.

Buildings in big cities are often illuminated with neon lights.

EL wire can be used to make lit-up clothing too.

LIGHT IN A TUBE

A real neon light is made using a glass tube with electrodes at the ends, attached to an electric circuit. Neon gas, or another gas, such as argon or xenon, is sealed inside the tube. When it's switched on, the flow of electricity makes the gas glow.

EL wire works in a different way. It contains a copper wire coated with a chemical that glows when an electric current passes through it. It's covered in coloured plastic tubing to give the wire its colour. As EL wire is flexible, it's easy to make into any shape you like.

LIGHT YOURSELF UP

Lit-up jackets or t-shirts are great for parties and for festivals, where it can be hard to find your friends and family in the dark. To make one, use a needle and thread to sew a length of EL wire to your garment in a pattern or shape. Position it so that some of the wire is spare at the end, and you can put the battery pack into a pocket.

GLOSSARY

animalcules A name invented by Antonie van Leeuwenhoek for the tiny creatures he saw using his microscope.

argon A type of gas used to make coloured electric tube lights.

axis The imaginary line between the north and south poles that the Earth spins around.

bacteria A type of tiny living thing that can be seen using a microscope.

camera obscura A dark chamber or room used to capture an image of the world outside it.

diffuse Spread out evenly.

electric current A flow of electricity.

electrode A part of an electric circuit that makes contact with a non-metallic substance, such as air.

EL wire Short for electroluminescent wire, a type of wire that glows when an electric current flows through it.

fibre-optic cable A cable containing fine, flexible glass tubes that light can travel along.

internal reflection The way light bounces off the inside of a fibre-optic cable or tube.

lens A curved, transparent object used to make light bend, or refract, as it passes through it.

light rays The straight paths that light waves follow as they travel forwards.

microbes Very small living things that can only be seen with a microscope.

microwaves A type of invisible light wave with a long wavelength.

neon A type of gas used to make coloured electric tube lights.

radio waves A type of invisible light wave with a very long wavelength.

reflection The way light bounces off surfaces, especially light or shiny surfaces such as a mirror.

refraction The way light can change direction as it passes from one transparent material into another.

retina The layer of light-sensitive cells inside the back of the eye.

solar power Energy from the sun that is collected and used to generate electricity or power machines.

solstice The summer solstice is the day of the year with the most hours of daylight, and the winter solstice is the day of the year with the fewest hours of daylight.

translucent Letting light through, but diffusing it so that objects are not clearly visible.

visible light The range of wavelengths of light that the human eye can detect.

wavelength The length of a light wave or other wave, measured from the top of one wave to the top of the next.

xenon A type of gas used to make coloured electric tube lights.

x-rays A type of invisible light wave with a short wavelength.

FURTHER INFORMATION

WEBSITES ABOUT LIGHT

Science Kids: Light
www.sciencekids.co.nz/light.html

Optics for Kids
optics.synopsys.com/learn/kids/optics-kids-light.html

Optics4Kids
www.optics4kids.org/home

Explain That Stuff! Light
www.explainthatstuff.com/light.html

WEBSITES ABOUT MAKING

Tate Kids: Make
www.tate.org.uk/kids/make

PBS Design Squad Global
pbskids.org/designsquad

Instructables
www.instructables.com

Make:
makezine.com

WHERE TO BUY MATERIALS

Maplin
For electronic components and making projects
www.maplin.co.uk

Hobbycraft
For art and craft materials
www.hobbycraft.co.uk

B&Q
For pipes, tubing, wood, glue and other hardware
www.diy.com

Fred Aldous
For art and craft materials, photography supplies and books
www.fredaldous.co.uk

BOOKS

BOOM! Science: Light by Georgia Amson-Bradshaw (Wayland, 2018)

Ludicrous Light (Strange Science and Explosive Experiments) by Mike Clark (The Secret Book Company, 2017)

Home Lab by Robert Winston and Jack Challoner (Dorling Kindersley, 2016)

Science in a Flash: Light by Georgia Amson-Bradshaw (Franklin Watts, 2017)

Tabletop Scientist: The Science of Light by Steve Parker (Dover Publications, 2013)

Tabletop Scientist: The Science of Air by Steve Parker (Dover Publications, 2013)

PLACES TO VISIT

National Science and Media Museum, Bradford, UK
www.scienceandmediamuseum.org.uk

Science Museum, London, UK
www.sciencemuseum.org.uk

Museum of Science and Industry, Manchester, UK
msimanchester.org.uk

Smithsonian National Air and Space Museum, Washington DC, USA
airandspace.si.edu

INDEX

DISCOVER MORE...

SCIENCE MAKERS

978 1 5263 0546 6

Understanding sound
Found sounds
Talk to the tube
It came from outer space!
AKB48 bottle train
Turn it up!
Underwater ear
Seeing sounds
Get into the groove
Sonic sculpture
Intruder alert!

978 1 5263 0542 8

Understanding forces
Speeding car stunt ramp
Newton's cradle
Making flight history
Pressure diver
Rocket power
Floating on air
Whale race
Pendulum art
Kinetic creations
Follow the force!

978 1 5263 0544 2

Understanding living things
Miniature plant world
Fast flowers
Colours of nature
Close-up creepy crawlies
Animal movement
Weave a web
Hear your heart
Body copy
Building blocks of life
Fabulous fossils

978 1 5263 0526 8

Understanding light
Art in shadows
A new view
Curved light
A closer look
Make the world upside-down
Sun prints
Painting with light
Garden gnomon
Lightbox display
Neon sign

978 1 5263 0550 3

Understanding machines
Thing flinger
Cable delivery!
Powered flight
Weather machine
Bubbles galore!
At the touch of a toe
Snack machine
Flapping bird
Vibrobot
Robot tentacle

978 1 5263 0548 0

Understanding states of matter
Chocolate art
Summer slushies
Crayon creations
Instant ice cream
Glue gun art
Melting ice people
Desert cooler
Save your life at sea
Evaporation art
Recycled paper

WAYLAND
www.waylandbooks.co.uk